Poulet, Virginia
    Blue bug's surprise. Illustrated by Mary
Maloney and Stan Fleming.   Chicago, Children
Press, [1977]
    29p.

    1.Flowers-Fiction.   I.Maloney, Mary P.
II.Fleming,Stanley.   III.Title.

BLUE BUG'S SURPRISE

By Virginia Poulet

Illustrated by Mary Maloney and Stan Fleming

 CHILDRENS PRESS, CHICAGO

Especially for my daughter, Cathy

Library of Congress Cataloging in Publication Data

Poulet, Virginia.
  Blue Bug's surprise.

  SUMMARY: Blue Bug surprises his friend by giving her
many kinds of flowers. Then she surprises him.
  [1. Flowers—Fiction] I. Maloney, Mary P.
II. Fleming, Stanley. III. Title.
PZ7.P86Bmr   [E]   76-50670
ISBN 0-516-03427-8

1 2 3 4 5 6 7 8 9 10 11 12 R 79 78 77

To surprise Feebee,
Blue Bug picked

4

a daisy

rose

forget-me-nots

petunia

12

snapdragon

13

14

marigold

tulip

pansy

geranium

peony

zinnia

and violets.

Blue Bug surprised Feebee.

Then Feebee surprised Blue Bug!